ABOUT THE STORY

"The Shine Around the Moon" grew out a sense of wonderment the author felt as a young child while viewing the glowing moon above her native island of Fiji. But as a child, she was bewildered by the moon's incredible light, not quite understanding how this could come about. Every night before she went to bed, she would gaze at the moon and ask her mother questions about the moon's shine and its light. She soon realized that this also helped to prolong her bedtime.

The author loved trying to touch the moon and actually thought she could as a child. Mostly, she enjoyed feeling a sense of loving and well being because the moon came out every night to shine for her and to let her love its great light. This was also a special time of sharing with her mother, a time when they could be alone in their thoughts. Her mother always answered the same questions with a smile, allowing her to believe in and to be awed by the moon's shine.

The green sea turtle below and on the back cover is a family pet named "Dinu" who still lives in a salt water pond just outside their house in Fiji. Throughout her life, the author's imagination has always kept her striving to reach the moon. The author hopes that the parents, teachers, and most importantly, the children who share in this story will continue to love the great shine around the moon and will each strive in their own way to reach the moon.

The Shine Around the Moon

To my best friend Jane Weber—
Thank you for your unconditional love, caring and an abundance of always believing in me.
This has led me to succeed and to exceed beyond my own imagination.
You are my family.
Love, Roshni

We all need someone to believe in us
as much as we believe in ourselves.

❧

Published by The Image Maker Publishing Co.
29417 Bluewater Rd. • Malibu, CA 90265

Text copyright © 1997 by Roshni Mangal
Illustrations copyright © 1997 by Maxwell Purple

Library of Congress Cataloging-in-Publication Data
Mangal, Roshni, 1963-
The Shine Around the Moon.
p. cm.
Summary: A young child asks her mother why the moon shines so bright
and whether the moon has a family like she does.
ISBN 0-9644695-2-9
[1. Astronomy–Fiction. 2. Family–Fiction. 3. Bedtime–Fiction.] I. Purple, Maxwell, ill. II. Title.
Printed in the U.S.A.
First Edition.
Guaranteed reinforced binding.

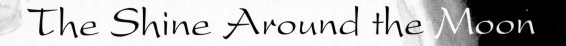

The Shine Around the Moon

Written by
Roshni Mangal

Illustrated by
Maxwell Purple

Image Maker Publishing
Malibu, CA

Every night before I go to bed, I ask my mother why the moon shines.

I ask my mother why
the moon is so bright.

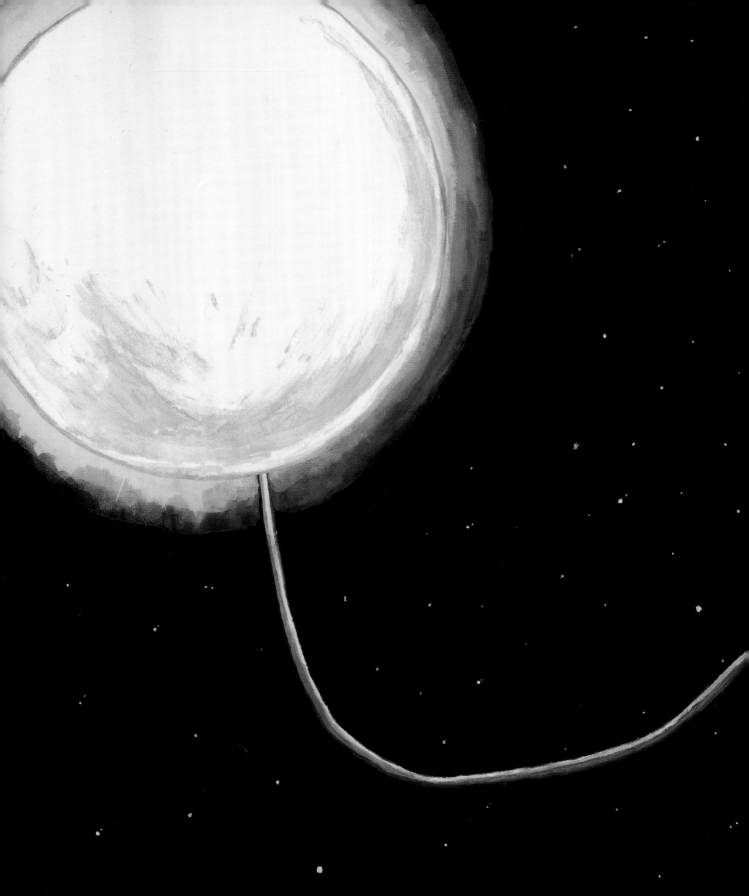

I ask my mother
if she plugs in the moon for me

so that I would have
a bright night light.

I ask my mother
if the moon has a family like I do.

My mother told me that the moon shines so bright because it's happy

that all the children
are going to bed tucked in,
all within it's great sight.

My mother told me that the moon is bright
and shines for me because

I appreciate its light
and its might.

My mother told me that she
does not plug in the moon because

it already has its very own
electricity and energy
that comes from
the moon's
insides —

like a heart...

in our bodies that
beats to keep us alive.

The moon's heart is a
bright shiny light that lights up

the sky and our world
outside.

My mother told me
that the moon

does have a family in the sky:

the billions of stars,
the many different planets,

the sun . . .

and all the children of the world —

they are the moon's family.

ABOUT THE AUTHOR

Ms. Roshni Mangal grew up in the Fiji Islands. She was born to parents of Indian and Welsh descent. English was the third language she learned as a child after Hindu and Fijian. She moved to the United States at the age of eleven and has been independent since the age of sixteen.

Ms. Mangal's many educational pursuits in the United States have included an Associate of Arts Degree in Liberal Studies and a Bachelor of Arts Degree in Child Development. She is currently completing a Master of Arts Degree specializing in Child Psychology. As a teacher of preschool children over the past fifteen years, her interests and hands-on experiences have led her to develop a particularly insightful interaction with children from ages three to six years.

The author is known for her boundless enthusiasm, commitment to excellence and concern for her students, as well as her insight and ability to communicate. She successfully instills an enthusiasm for learning in her students, allowing them to exceed what might normally be expected of preschool education. Furthermore, the respect she shows her students and their families reflects upon the optimism and commitment she has for their future.

Ms. Mangal applies her dedication, determination, and pursuit of excellence in both her personal and professional life. This author's door is always open to those who seek guidance and someone who cares. In working with many diverse groups of students and parents over the years, the author has learned to adapt to the many obstacles and challenges she has faced and to turn them, instead, into opportunities for growth and understanding.

ABOUT THE ILLUSTRATOR

Maxwell Purple grew up in California and has been a practicing artist and writer for most of his life, beginning to draw at a very early age. Much of his work has been self-taught and self-directed, although he has studied life drawing at the American Animation Institute.

The illustrations for "The Shine Around the Moon" were done in gouache watercolors on paper. In them, Purple states that he tried to convey the "quiet loudness" of the moon in the night sky. He has often chosen to paint the rising moon over the Pacific Ocean, fascinated with the interplay between the moon's light on the water and the ocean's mist.

The illustrator has enjoyed leading artistic activities for preschool children in the past, noting that they always put emotion into everything they do. His other artistic endeavors have included graphic design work and album cover illustration for several bands and other organizations, and work as a performance artist while reading his poetry.